★ BASEBALL BUDDIES ★

Building a Team

★ BASEBALL BUDDIES ★

BOOK 1

Building a Team

by Aaron Derr
Illustrations by Gary LaCoste

RED CHAIR PRESS

Egremont, Massachusetts

RED CHAIR PRESS
BOOKS FOR YOUNG READERS

www.redchairpress.com

Publisher's Cataloging-In-Publication Data
(Provided by Cassidy Cataloging Services, Inc.)

Names: Derr, Aaron, author. | LaCoste, Gary, illustrator.

Title: Baseball buddies : building a team / by Aaron Derr ; illustrations by Gary LaCoste.

Other Titles: Building a team

Description: Egremont, Massachusetts : Red Chair Press, [2024] | Interest age level: 007-010. | Summary: When Luis joins his new baseball team, the Manatees, things seem pretty hopeless at first. Some of his new teammates ... are mean to him or to each other. His new coach doesn't tell the players everything to do like his old coach did. And some of the Manatees seem more interested in goofing off than in sportsmanship or working hard. Then Coach Joe makes Luis team captain. Will Luis rise to the challenge? Can he get the Manatees to balance working hard and having fun? Will he help his teammates learn to be friends rather than compete with each other?--Publisher.

Identifiers: ISBN: 978-164371-284-0 (hardcover) | 978-1-64371-286-4 (multi-user ebook PDF) | 978-1-64371-287-1 (ePub3 S&L) | 978-1-64371-288-8 (ePub3 TR) | 978-1-64371-289-5 (Kf8) | LCCN: 2022949359

Subjects: LCSH: Baseball--Juvenile fiction. | Teamwork (Sports)--Juvenile fiction. | Self-esteem in children--Juvenile fiction. | Friendship--Juvenile fiction. | Bullying--Juvenile fiction. | CYAC: Baseball--Fiction. | Teamwork (Sports)--Fiction. | Self-esteem--Fiction. | Friendship--Fiction. | Bullies and bullying-Fiction. | LCGFT: Sports fiction. | BISAC: JUVENILE FICTION / Sports & Recreation / Baseball & Softball. | JUVENILE FICTION / Social Themes / Self-Esteem & Self-Reliance. | JUVENILE FICTION / Social Themes / Peer Pressure.

Classification: LCC: PZ7.1.D4687 Ba 2024 | DDC: [Fic]--dc23

Main body text set in Amasis Regular 17/27

Printed in Canada

1023 1P S24FN

MIX
Paper from
responsible sources
FSC® C016245

For my kids,
who in one way or another
have inspired every one of my stories.
—Aaron

From the moment he first laid eyes on him, Luis knew he wasn't going to like Jimmie. Luis was the new kid on the team, and it was the first day of baseball practice.

"Hey boys, everybody say 'hi' to Luis," said their coach. "He's a terrific baseball player, and I'm thrilled to have him on our team!"

"I don't think he said 'terrific,' " said Luis's friend. "I think he said 'average.' "

"Haha," said Luis. "I'm not going to tell the story if you keep interrupting."

"Fine."

"He's a terrific baseball player, and I'm thrilled to have him on our team!"

Luis stopped for a second and looked at his

friend.

Luis's friend shrugged his shoulders as if to say, "whatever."

Most of the players on Luis's new team were nice to him. Especially Gary.

"I like this part," Gary whispered to Aliyah.

But not Jimmie.

Luis and Jimmie could not have been more different. Luis was skinny but fast. Jimmie was strong but slow. Luis was shy and quiet. Jimmie was loud and obnoxious.

"Loud and obnoxious?!?" laughed Luis's friend.

"Well, you are!" said Luis.

Jimmie loved to hear Luis tell this story. Which was kind of weird, because it was a story about him. And it was about Luis, too. And Gary. And Aliyah and Roberto. And all their other teammates.

At the other end of the dugout, a handful of players started collecting their gear. The ones who took care to keep their stuff organized—batting gloves, fielding mitts and the most important piece of gear of them all, bubble gum—were ready in no time. The rest were going to need just a few more minutes.

They were the McIntyre Manatees—named after one of the most unusual animals in the world. McIntyre was the name of the neighborhood where they all lived. Manatees are aquatic animals that are kind of weird and funny looking, but also smart and capable of learning from their mistakes.

Seriously. It was the perfect mascot for this team.

The time to go out to the field hadn't yet arrived, but it was getting close.

"Do you guys remember when Jimmie tried to teach Luis how to hit a home run?" said Gary. "And Jimmie was totally like…"

"HEY!" Jimmie yelled.

Everyone went quiet.

"Let Luis tell the story! He tells it best!"

No one dared speak. Even the players at the other end of the dugout stopped what they were doing. Everyone looked at Jimmie.

"Uhm, Jimmie?" Luis said softly. "We've talked about this."

Jimmie nodded his head.

"Right," he said. "Sorry. Sorry, Gary. Sorry, everybody!"

Jimmie leaned forward and apologized to the teammates on his left. Then he did the same to his teammates on the right.

Luis nodded.

Jimmie looked at Luis and took a deep breath, and when he spoke again, he was like a completely different kid.

"Hey guys," he said softly. "Do you think maybe we could let Luis tell the story? I just think he tells it best."

Luis looked at Gary, who could barely contain his laughter.

Aliyah didn't bother trying not to laugh. She just laughed out loud.

"Sure, Jimmie," Gary said. "Let's let Luis tell it."

"Thank you," said Jimmie, politely.

"You're welcome," said Gary, just as politely.

Everyone relaxed.

Some of the players began peeking their heads outside the dugout to get a good look at the sky. The rain was definitely starting to let up now. The worst of the storm clouds were moving away from them. Some specks of blue sky were already creeping through the few clouds that remained.

Some of Luis's teammates were now standing at the dugout's exit, waiting to be cleared to run onto the field. Others were still scrambling to find their missing batting gloves, or—more likely— that one last piece of bubble gum.

"If I'm going to tell the story, I have to tell the whole story, going back to our first practice," Luis said.

"Oh, brother," Jimmie said, rolling his eyes.

At their first practice, it was obvious that Luis and Jimmie were going to be trouble. The first time Luis bobbled a grounder, Jimmie said—with tremendous sarcasm—"Nice job."

And the first time Jimmie dropped a throw from Luis, Luis said, "Great catch."

"OK now you're exaggerating I don't think I—"

The kids who were still nearby all looked at Jimmie.

He looked back at them.

"Fine," he said softly.

"Hey!" said their coach. "The weather's looking better. Let's get loosened up!"

The players all looked at one another and smiled, then grabbed their gear and ran onto the field.

They were good friends, and good teammates, too. Win or lose, they always had each other's backs.

But it wasn't always that way.

CHAPTER 1

If you're a baseball player, springtime is the best time. There's just no doubt about it.

Football players have autumn, with the changing leaves and cooling temperatures. Basketball and hockey players have winter, with their indoor games played in heated arenas.

But baseball? Baseball simply owns the spring. Yes, baseball season goes on throughout the summer. And if you make it to the Majors, you might be playing right up to the edge of fall.

But if you're 11 years old, and you play baseball, spring is where it's at. After a long winter away from the game, everyone is happy to be back. Everyone is excited. No one has even lost a game yet!

Yep, Luis thought. This is it. This is where I want to be. These are the best days of my—

"Luis! What are you doing over there? Why are you staring at the sky? We're having a team meeting over here! Do you want to be part of this team, or not?"

Luis shook himself awake from his daydream. After having moved from Texas to Ohio, Luis often thought about his old friends back in Texas. His new coach—Coach Joe was his name— was halfway across the field. The players were beginning to gather around Coach Joe for the meeting. Some had already taken a knee, ready to listen to whatever guidance their leader had to offer.

Luis had lost track of time and fallen behind.

"Right, coach! Sorry! Coming!"

Luis hustled over to join his teammates. Not a great start to his first practice with his new team, but that's OK. He'd have plenty of chances to show his new coach that he was willing to do whatever was asked of him.

"Here I am, the perfect follower," Luis thought. "Whatever you say, coach, I'll do it."

Luis was going to make the best out of this situation.

He missed his old team and his old coach. Coach Terry always told them exactly what to do.

"Stand over here."

"Hit the ball over there."

"Relax, you're too tense."

"Straighten up, you're too relaxed!"

But Coach Terry had to go and take a job in another city, and he took his two baseball-playing daughters with him. Everyone was kind of left on their own to find a new team—and a new coach. And then Luis's dad got a new job in Ohio.

And now, Luis had Coach Joe.

It was Luis's mom who found the Manatees, a community team of boys and girls from around the neighborhood. Weird mascot, but whatever. The mascot didn't matter. What mattered was how you played the game. Luis's mom says the other parents wouldn't stop talking about how much they love this coach. She knew some of them from school and others from the neighborhood, and she trusted their opinions.

OK, fine, thought Luis. I'll do my best. Keep a positive attitude. Work hard. Do whatever he says. Show him I can be a good follower. What else am I going to do, quit baseball?

That wasn't an option, of course.

Luis sat down on the outer edge of the circle of players. Most of them appeared to know each other already.

"OK everybody," said Coach Joe. "Welcome to another baseball season with the Manatees!"

Coach Joe paused as if he was expecting everyone to cheer or clap or something.

No one did, except one kid wearing catcher's gear, who clapped twice, said "yay!" kind of softly, looked around and realized no one else was doing it, then immediately stopped.

"OK," coach Joe continued. "Thank you, Gary, for clapping there. Seems like maybe last year's team would have applauded more. It's fine. You guys are just getting older, I guess. Too cool for that kind of stuff now. Good. Well... if you played for us last year, welcome back. We're glad to have you here. Again. With... us. The team.

"And if you're new, I'm Coach Joe."

Coach Joe waited again as if he was expecting someone to say something, like "Hi Coach Joe!" Or "Yay Coach Joe!" Or something.

No one said anything, except the kid in the

catcher's gear, who said, so faintly you could barely hear it, "Hi Coach Joe."

It seemed like it took forever for Coach Joe to figure out what he was going to say next. Some

of the players shifted from one knee to the other. Others just looked around nervously.

Was Coach Joe about to say something… important?

"OK. Yes. Well, it seems like this team might be a little bit different than last year's. Which is fine, because I want you guys to know I'm going to do things a little bit different than you might be used to. Everyone is a year older now, and it's time for the players—not the coach—to lead this team. When you were little, you needed a coach to tell you every single thing to do. Well, you aren't little anymore. Most of you, at least."

Coach Joe chuckled a bit and waited for someone to laugh.

No one did. Not even Gary the catcher.

"Wow. OK. Right. So, the first thing we're going to do, before we start practice, is name our team captain. Now, I'm here to tell you, anybody can be team captain. It doesn't matter if you were here last year, or if you're new this year. The future is wide open for all of you."

This seemed to get everyone's attention.

All the players who were slouched over before suddenly sat up straight.

"What does the team captain have to do?" asked a girl who was sitting right next to Coach Joe.

"Wow! Finally! Someone spoke up! This is great!" said Coach Joe.

"I actually said something two times," said Gary, but it was so quiet that Coach Joe didn't hear him.

"I'm glad you asked that question, Aliyah. So, listen. I'm still the coach. I'm going to set the practice schedule. I'm going to decide what kind of drills we do in practice. I'm going to set the lineup. Decide who pitches. All of that. But the team captain? Well, the team captain maybe has an even more important job than mine."

Coach Joe paused, waiting for someone to ask, "What job is that, Coach Joe?"

No one said anything.

Gary, the kid in the catcher's gear, looked like he really wanted to say something, but then thought better of it.

Coach Joe, clearly disappointed, shook his head.

"My gosh, what in the…" Coach Joe's voice trailed off. He put his hand on his forehead.

"OK, listen. So, that job is, making sure we practice the *right* way," he said. "Making sure we do our drills the *right* way. Making sure we have a good attitude. And being the person that your teammates can talk to if they have a problem. Maybe calling a players-only meeting, if they want to talk about things."

This is different, thought Luis.

"Isn't that *your* job, Coach?" said the biggest kid on the team, maybe the biggest kid Luis had seen in his whole life. I mean, this kid was so big, it seemed like there was no way he was the same age as the rest of the players. He was a different species almost.

"Another question! Wow! That's two in one meeting! This is going great!" said Coach Joe. "But seriously, I'm glad you asked that question, Jimmie. All the best teams in every sport have good team captains. A coach can only do so much. When you get to a certain age, you need to have a leader who's also one of your teammates. Because whatever the message is, it means more coming from that person than it would from me."

Coach Joe paused to see if anyone else was going to ask a question.

No one did. But they were all paying attention. That's for sure. The ones who weren't really interested earlier? Well, they were interested now, absolutely. It seemed like maybe everyone thought being team captain would be pretty cool.

But Luis didn't think it'd be cool at all. He was a follower, not a leader.

"So, this is what we're going to do. We're going to go around our little circle here. Every player is going to introduce themselves. Everyone is going to tell us what they like about baseball. Then I'm going to tell you who's going to be our team captain."

Oh boy. This is *really* different, thought Luis. This just got real.

Luis wasn't particularly worried. Surely, he'd have a few minutes until it was his turn. He would just listen to what the other kids said, then take something that sounded good and change it up just enough so that—

"Luis," said Coach Joe. "Since you were the last one here, you get to go first."

Oh great. This would never have happened if I had just paid attention, thought Luis.

★ CHAPTER 2 ★

"**H**ey guys, everybody say 'hi' to Luis," said Coach Joe. "He's a terrific baseball player—or so his mom tells me."

This got a giggle from a few of the players. Not as many as Coach Joe would have liked, but it was better than nothing.

"Seriously though, I'm thrilled to have him on our team."

This got a giant chuckle—more like a snort, really—from the big kid. Coach Joe said his name was Jimmie. Well, when Jimmie chuckled, it sounded like a big old bear snorting.

"Hi everybody," Luis said. He did his best to sound strong and confident, but he wasn't sure if he came across that strong and confident to everybody else.

"I'm Luis," he said.

"Yeah, we got that part already!" yelled Jimmie.

"Hey Jimmie," said Coach Joe. "Let's show some respect to our teammates, OK buddy? You never know. Luis might be our team captain."

Jimmie didn't say anything, but Luis saw him roll his eyes.

"Uhh… My name's Luis…"

Darn it, I already said that, thought Luis.

"And I… uhhh… I played for the Galveston Beach Sharks last year. So… kind of funny. From the Sharks to the Manatees. But uhhh… anyway…"

Luis was starting to panic.

"I normally play shortstop, but you know… I'll play wherever.… And uhhh… you know… I'm just happy to be here. And…"

100 percent panic mode now.

"And what I like about baseball is, you know… well… uhm… I just hope we have a lot of fun."

That was a stupid thing to say, thought Luis.

Coach Joe looked at Luis for several seconds. Luis couldn't tell if he was confused or what.

"Huh," said Coach Joe. "Interesting. That's not what I was expecting."

Luis looked down at his shoes. Then across the field at some trees.

"Tell me this, Luis," said Coach Joe. "Aren't you afraid that if all your teammates just want to have fun, that they won't care enough about winning? That maybe they won't work hard enough in practice to become better players?"

"Well," said Luis. "I mean... I guess so... but uhm..."

"And what would you do if that were to happen?" said Coach Joe. "What would you do if your teammates were having *too* much fun? What if they were just joking around, laughing all the time, not really working hard on being good baseball players?"

"Well," said Luis. "I guess I'd... uhm..."

He was really struggling now.

"I guess I'd just uhm... maybe talk to them all? Make sure they knew that it's OK to have fun as long as you're also working hard?"

Luis didn't look at his teammates, but he felt like they were probably all just as confused as he was.

"OK," said Joe. "That's interesting.

"Aliyah, why don't you go next."

And so it went on. One by one, Luis's new teammates introduced themselves and said what they like about baseball.

But no one quite answered the question like Luis did.

There was Aliyah, the center fielder who jumped to her feet right away with incredible enthusiasm. She said what she liked about baseball was stealing bases. Because she was so fast, she made it look easy.

There was Gary, the catcher, who said what he liked about baseball was trying to throw out runners who were trying to steal a base. Then he admitted he'd never actually done that in a game before.

Gary looked at Aliyah shyly, and she grinned and gave him a little fist bump.

"You'll get one this year, Gary," said Aliyah. "I know you will."

There was Roberto, who also claimed to be a center fielder. He said what he liked most about baseball was playing center field, not right field. It seemed like his voice kind of got louder and louder as he said it.

And Luis noticed that he looked right at Aliyah when he said it, but Aliyah looked the other direction.

There was Lisa, the pitcher, who said what she liked about baseball was striking out every batter in an inning. Then doing it again the next inning. Then doing it again and again. She laughed, and so did some of the other players.

And, finally, when everyone else had finished, there was Jimmie, the gigantic first baseman. He didn't seem as positively enthusiastic as the others, but Luis could tell he was putting some thought into what he was going to say.

"What I like about baseball is bashing home runs so hard they fly up into the sky and never come down," he said.

Several of the players laughed a little bit, but it wasn't like they were making fun of Jimmie. Luis figured they wouldn't dare. Jimmie could stomp them all if he wanted to.

When Jimmie was done, Coach Joe spoke again.

"OK! Great job everybody! Those are some excellent thoughts there," he said. "I'm going to have to think long and hard about who's going to be the team captain. Oh wait, I just decided!"

Everyone got quiet. Like, super quiet. Like, quieter than they had been since they woke up that morning. Then, Coach Joe spoke.

"Congratulations, Luis! You're our new team captain!"

★ CHAPTER 3 ★

"**W**ait. What?" said Luis.

He wasn't sure if he had heard correctly. Surely, he hadn't heard correctly.

"Coach, I really don't know…" said Luis.

"Ha ha ha… duh… Coach, I really don't know!"

It was Jimmie making fun of Luis, but Jimmie was the least of Luis's problems now. His top priority at this moment was to make this whole captain thing go away.

"All right, everybody," said Coach Joe. "That's enough of my yappin'. Let's get this practice started. Defense wins championships, so everybody… get to your positions… it's time to practice ground balls and pop flies."

The Manatees did as they were told—some more enthusiastically than others—but Luis didn't move. Some of his teammates stared at him as they walked past. Some seemed jealous. Others seemed mad. Some seemed more... curious.

Jimmie walked by without acknowledging him at all.

"Hi captain!"

It was Gary, the catcher, and his enthusiasm startled Luis.

"I'm Gary!"

He reached out to shake Luis's hand. Luis took his hand and shook it, a little nervously.

"Hey Gary," said Luis. "It's nice to meet you. But listen…"

Luis leaned in, as if to tell Gary a secret.

"I'm not gonna—"

"Oh, you're gonna, all right," said Gary, still shaking Luis's hand. "I guess when Coach Joe makes a decision, it sticks. You're our captain. No question about it."

"You mean sucks," said Luis.

"Don't worry! You'll do great! Let me know what I can do to help!"

Luis just stood there as Gary trotted off to take his position behind home plate. It took Luis a second to realize he was still moving his hand up and down, as if he was still shaking hands with Gary.

Almost everyone had gotten to their positions now, including Coach Joe, who was standing near Gary at home plate. He was getting ready to start hitting practice balls to everybody.

"Uhh, captain?" said Coach Joe. "I need you to head out to your position. We're taking grounders and pop-ups."

"But coach, I... uhh..."

"Captain," said Coach Joe, more seriously than Luis had seen him so far. "Get to your position. Defense wins championships, and I need my shortstop to be good on defense."

Luis nodded, grabbed his glove, and trotted out to shortstop.

"OK everybody!" yelled Coach Joe, now standing in the batter's box and resting a baseball bat on his shoulder. "I hereby pronounce that baseball season has begun. Here's the situation: Top of the first inning, nobody out, nobody on. Leadoff batter at the plate. Think about what you do if the ball's hit toward you."

Coach Joe pointed to his head with the hand that wasn't holding the bat when he said this.

"Be ready, everybody. Eyes up!"

"Eyes up!" yelled all the returning members of the Manatees, who seemed to already know this routine.

Coach Joe took a baseball from the bag of gear laying on the ground next to him, tossed it up in the air... and batted a scorching ground ball right at Luis.

Luis bobbled it. Because of course he did. First ground ball of the year, hit right at him, in front of all of his teammates... of course he did.

"Nice job!" yelled Jimmie from first base.

But the ball didn't roll far away. Luis scrambled to retrieve it as quickly as he could, then fired a rocket over to first base.

The speed of the throw seemed to take Jimmie by surprise. It hit him right in the soft part of his glove... then bounced right back out.

"Great catch," said Luis.

Jimmie looked angry.

For the next hour and-a-half, the Manatees worked on just about every baseball situation imaginable. Runner on first with one out? They worked on that. Runners on first and third with two outs? They worked on that, too. Bases loaded with nobody out? Of course they worked on that.

Coach Joe made them work on more situations than it seemed could possibly exist in the game of baseball.

After bobbling the first ball hit at him, Luis handled the rest like it was no problem. Line drives, slow rollers, pop-ups… he grabbed them all, firing the ball to first base when he had to, each time with pinpoint accuracy.

And Jimmie, to his credit, was pretty good, too. He took his share of grounders, and caught every throw from Luis, even a few that were in the dirt.

"I like this combination!" said Coach Joe at one point. "Luis at short and Jimmie at first! You guys are doing awesome!"

Neither Luis nor Jimmie looked at each other.

Finally, just as Luis felt like his arm was about to fall off, Coach Joe declared practice to be over. He called everyone together for one last meeting for the day.

"This team sure does have a lot of meetings,"

Luis said to the girl named Aliyah, but she didn't say anything back.

"Good practice everybody!" said Coach Joe. "Really happy with how hard everybody worked today. And it seems like our new player is fitting in just fine."

He looked at Luis when he said that, but Luis just looked at the back of the head of the teammate in front of him.

"Captain? You got anything to say?" Coach Joe asked.

All the players turned and looked at Luis. Every. Single. One of them.

"Uhm," Luis said.

He heard someone snicker. Probably Jimmie but he couldn't say for sure. And he didn't have time to worry about it anyway.

"Not really. Good job, everybody?"

But Luis said it more like a question than a statement.

Coach Joe smiled.

"OK. That's fine, Luis. Everybody go home and get some rest. We'll see you all tomorrow."

After all the other kids had either left or were on their way out toward the parking lot, Luis saw Coach Joe picking up some stray water bottles near one of the dugouts.

This was his chance.

"Some of you left your water bottles!" Coach Joe yelled. "Come get 'em before I keep 'em!"

Gary, all the way out in the parking lot, with one foot in his parents' car, somehow heard.

"Oof!" said Gary. "Sorry coach! Coming!"

And he began jogging all the way back to the practice field to get his bottle.

"Coach… seriously… real quick," said Luis.

Coach Joe looked at Luis and let out a sigh.

"OK, Luis," said Coach Joe. "Let's talk about it."

Coach Joe sat down on the bench.

"I can't do it," said Luis. "I… I'm not a captain. I've never been a captain. I don't know what to do!"

"Luis, I wouldn't have asked you to be captain

if I didn't believe that you could do it."

"But Coach! You don't even know me!"

"I learned all I needed to know about you by the way you answered that question. Do you realize what you said?"

"I just said I wanted to have fun!"

"Yes! That's exactly right! Because that's what baseball's all about! It's about working hard, sure. And it's about trying to win, sure. I'm in favor of both of those things. Especially the part about winning. Nobody likes winning more than me.

"But what baseball is really about is having fun while you're doing all those other things. If we all aren't having fun, what's the point? And you're the only one who said that.

"Everyone else talked about themselves, and what they liked about baseball for themselves. You're the only one who talked about the team."

"Well, yeah, I guess, but..."

Luis was beginning to lose hope that he was going to be able to get out of this. He looked at the ground. He shook his head. He looked at the sky. He shook his head again.

"Did you mean it?" said Coach Joe.

"What?" said Luis.

"Did you mean what you said? About having fun? About making sure your teammates have fun while also working hard?"

Luis thought for a second. Was this his chance to get out of it? To just say that he panicked, that he didn't know what to say, that he just made it all up?

He felt like he had been given a chance to get out of being team captain, and all he had to do was take advantage of it, and then he could be done with it. All he had to say was, "No, I didn't mean it. I just said it because I couldn't think of anything else."

But he couldn't do it, because it wouldn't be the truth. He had meant what he said. Sure, it just came out because he was nervous, but he still meant it.

Luis sighed. He couldn't believe he was about to say what he was about to say.

"Yeah, I meant it," he said, now fully realizing that he was going to be the team captain, like it or not.

Coach Joe nodded.

"Yep, that's what I thought," he said, and he stood up, grabbed his bag of baseball gear, and began to walk out.

That was it. That was his chance to get out of this, and he couldn't take it. There was no going back now.

"Your job as captain is going to be to make sure everyone is having fun while also working hard," said Coach Joe. "That's the really tricky part. That's probably the hardest part of coaching. That's what I need you to do. That's what I need from my team captain. I can't wait to see how you handle it!"

"But… wait," said Luis. "How will I know? How will I know if they're having too much fun… or, not enough fun… or… not working hard enough?"

"You'll know, Luis."

Gary finally got all the way back to the practice field. Coach Joe gave him his water bottle and said, "Good practice, Gary. See you tomorrow."

"Thanks Coach," he said. Then he looked at Luis. "Good practice, captain!"

Luis waived at him, and Gary ran back toward the parking lot. Coach Joe headed that way, too, only a little bit slower.

After a few steps, Coach Joe stopped and turned around.

Luis was still standing there.

"Eyes up, Luis," he said. "You can do this. You just don't know it yet."

★ CHAPTER 4 ★

The Manatees had three weeks to get ready for their first game.

They had a lot of work to do.

Their first few practices focused almost only on what Coach Joe called "the fundamentals of defense." They practiced throwing the ball to the right person. They practiced covering the right base. And they practiced helping out a teammate who made a mistake. In other words, the boring stuff.

During fielding practice, Coach Joe would always do all the hitting himself. He would toss the ball up in the air with one hand before whacking it out of the air with a bat in his other hand. He was really good at hitting the ball right where he wanted it to go. He liked to make sure that everybody got a turn to try and catch it.

So, it made sense that he would be the one doing the hitting during that part of practice.

But when hitting practice finally did roll around, boy, that was the fun part of baseball. Hitting against a real pitcher!

Lisa almost always pitched first, but she kept striking everyone out, so they had to let someone else go.

"Lisa!" yelled Coach Joe. "What did I tell you about striking out your teammates?"

"To do it all day every day?" Lisa replied.

"Exactly right," said Coach Joe. "Good job. Now take a break. Anthony! Your turn to pitch!"

It was much easier to hit when Anthony pitched. He was a nice kid. But nowhere near as good of a pitcher as Lisa. That's why Coach Joe liked Anthony to pitch to his teammates in practice. He threw the ball well enough to challenge every batter, but not like Lisa—who threw it so well that no one could hit it.

Coach Joe didn't want Lisa to take it easy

on anybody. He said he didn't want her to lose her "edge." And Lisa was fine with that. She seemed to enjoy striking everyone out, even her own teammates.

Jimmie, after taking three giant swings and misses against Lisa, walked back to the dugout with his head hung low. For a moment, Luis felt sorry for him, like the poor guy didn't realize this was just practice and didn't even count.

But once Anthony started pitching, everything changed. Luis knocked several line drives to left-center and right-center. Jimmie whacked a couple of mammoth home runs to left. Aliyah had some solid hits. She also hit some very soft ground balls, which were just as good as hits because she was so fast, nobody could throw her out.

Luis wondered if she was doing that on purpose or not, but then decided it didn't really matter.

And Gary? Well, Gary wasn't much of a hitter, it looked like.

Outside of Jimmie, Roberto was probably the team's top hitter. He didn't mash the ball like

Jimmie did, but he hit it plenty hard. He wasn't as fast as Aliyah, but he was still pretty darn fast. When he took the field, though, Roberto clearly wasn't happy. His position was right field, but Luis noticed him constantly looking toward Aliyah in center.

One time, with Anthony pitching, Jimmie hit a high, towering fly ball to deep left-center. Aliyah chased back after it and ran and ran and ran until she finally made an excellent catch. Roberto, from way over in right field, said "whatever" just loud enough for some of his teammates to hear him. But it wasn't loud enough for Coach Joe or Aliyah to hear.

After every practice, Coach Joe would call Luis over and ask him what he thought about the work the team had done that day. And every time, Luis would say something simple like, "Looked pretty good to me," or "Not bad, not bad at all."

And Joe would look at Luis for a second, then just say "OK, Luis. Good job today." And then practice would *really* be over.

Now, even the best baseball teams sometimes have practices where they don't do so well. But this would always make Coach Joe grumpy. And when Coach Joe would get grumpy, he would make the players do more defensive drills. And that would make the players grumpy, because that would mean none of them would get to practice hitting.

If Coach Joe wasn't careful, before he knew it, everyone would be grumpy.

"Luis! What are you thinking?" Coach Joe would say. "Why would you throw the ball to second when you could have gotten the runner out at home?" Or "Jimmie! You have got to hustle after the ball when it gets away from you. You're just giving the other team extra bases!"

Well, during one particular practice, Coach Joe had had enough. He had been hitting balls to his fielders for almost an hour, and no one seemed to be able to do anything right. Luis had dropped a ball at shortstop. Jimmie had let a ball go right through his legs at first base. And even Aliyah hadn't hustled after a soft fly ball like she should have.

Just before it was time to practice hitting, Coach Joe shut everything down. He called the team together halfway between home plate and the pitcher's mound. The Manatees obediently gathered around their coach, but they weren't happy about it.

"Guys, we're just not playing smart baseball right now," he said. "There's no way around it. Our first game is coming up soon. I know these drills seem boring to you. But we aren't going to win many games until we get this stuff right."

Coach Joe looked at the baseball players gathered around him. Some were looking at the ground. Others were whispering and joking with each other. Others were just kind of staring off into the distance, as if they were already tired of baseball.

"Why is no one paying attention!?" he yelled.

Then he threw up his hands and let out a huge sigh.

"I don't know what to say, guys."

He looked at Luis and got an idea.

"Luis? Do you have anything to say to the team?"

"Uhm…"

It seemed to be Luis's favorite thing to say these days.

But then Luis looked over and saw a couple of his teammates whispering to each other. He saw a few more trying to sneak a peek at their phones. He thought about how he, himself, had been bored during practice today. Maybe he, too, had not been trying as hard as he should have.

And he decided, right then and there, that it was time for him to say something.

Luis walked into the center of the circle of baseball players and stood next to his coach.

"Guys, Coach is right," he said. "We haven't taken practice as seriously as we should have today."

Luis felt like the players all at once stopped looking at the ground. They stopped staring off in the distance. They stopped trying to peek at their phones.

All eyes were on him.

"That's exactly right," said Coach Joe, pointing at Luis. "Thank you! Listen to your captain, guys. He's exactly right."

Everyone was looking at Luis.

"I have an idea," said Luis.

"Good," said Coach Joe. "I want to hear this. Tell 'em your idea, captain."

Luis turned to face Coach Joe.

"Coach, we need to practice hitting."

"That's exactly— Hang on a second what did you just say?"

A handful of the players cheered. Others clapped.

"Hitting?" said Coach Joe. "We can't practice hitting until we learn how to field!"

"I understand," said Luis. "That's why I propose a compromise."

Now he had everyone's attention, for sure. Even Coach Joe had no idea what was coming next.

"I know why you like to hit balls when we practice fielding," said Luis. "And usually, it makes sense. You can hit it wherever you want, and you can make sure everybody gets enough chances to practice catching it.

"But, just this once, let's try something different," said Luis. "Instead of you hitting balls to us over and over and over again, let us practice hitting to each other against real pitching. I know it won't be as good as when you hit it to us. I mean, when Jimmie hits, we probably aren't going to get much fielding practice in, because all he does is hit home runs."

Luis laughed as he said this, and most of his teammates did, too. Luis looked at Jimmie just long enough to notice that Jimmie was smiling, even though he was trying not to.

"And when Lisa pitches, heck, she's probably going to strike us all out, but still…"

"Darn right," said Lisa, and again, everyone laughed.

Then Luis got serious.

"For this to work, I need whoever isn't hitting to be in your positions in the field, hustling after every ball," he said.

One by one, the players began nodding in agreement.

"I need you all to focus. I need you to pay attention. We need to get better at this."

All the players were nodding now. It seemed like they agreed with their captain.

Then Luis turned back to his coach.

"What do you say, Coach?"

Coach Joe thought about it. He looked at the players and noticed that every single one of them was paying attention now.

"This wasn't exactly what I had in mind when I asked you to be captain," he said to Luis, so softly that no one else could hear.

Luis smiled.

"You said what baseball is really about is having fun, right?" Luis said in a whisper. "I think, for now at least, we need to make baseball more fun."

Coach Joe seemed to realize that Luis had him on that one.

Then, louder, so everyone could hear, Coach Joe said, "OK, captain. Sounds like a plan."

"OK," said Luis. "Let's go, everybody. Eyes up."

CHAPTER 5

The Manatees won their first game 10–0, but Luis knew shortly after that something was wrong.

Lisa struck out two batters or more in every inning. Jimmie hit two monster home runs. And Luis himself had two hits and made several good plays at shortstop.

The team did well, no question about it. You don't win 10–0 without doing pretty darn good.

But Luis could tell that the team they were playing against just wasn't that strong. They had a lot of players who seemed to have way less experience than the Manatees. Luis heard Coach Joe talking to the coach of the other team after the game. The other coach said this was his first time coaching, and the first time a lot of his players had ever played in a real game.

A lot of them didn't even know where to go for the handshake line when it was all over.

So, while 10–0 is pretty good, Luis knew it was just one game. They still had a long season in front of them.

The thing is, he wasn't sure if his teammates felt the same way.

Ever since Luis had come up with that compromise with Coach Joe, practices had been going pretty well. The Manatees had gotten pretty good at defense. Sometimes, Coach Joe even let them spend an entire practice doing nothing but batting. It was great!

Coach Joe was still in charge, for sure. But sometimes Luis would point out some things that he thought could help, too. Usually, it was just repeating things he'd heard from Coach Joe and his other coaches over the years. But for some reason, when he said them, his teammates would listen.

Then they won 10–0, and something changed.

He decided to talk to Coach Joe about it on

the walk to the parking lot.

"Interesting," said Coach Joe. "We just won our first game 10–0, and you're telling me you feel like something isn't right?"

"I know. I'm probably being silly."

"Well, maybe you're not," said Coach Joe. "If you feel that way, maybe there's a reason for it. Try to be more specific, Luis. What is it exactly that doesn't feel right? Think about it."

"Well," said Luis. "I think it's the way we practice. It's fun. It's definitely fun. But we've had two practices since we won our first game, and it just feels like… I don't know. Like we aren't really trying very hard anymore. I mean, before the first game, we were having fun, but we were still trying hard. Now, we're still doing the fun part, but we're leaving out the trying hard part."

"I knew you would know," said Coach Joe.

"What?"

"I knew you would know when the team was having *too* much fun at practice. Remember? This is what I was talking about. I knew you would know.

"Now comes the hard part."

Luis stared at his coach.

"Look, this happens all the time," said Coach Joe. "Every season. Sometimes more than once in the same season. It takes a really smart kid to notice it, though, especially when you're right in the middle of it.

"I'm proud of you, Luis."

"Really?"

"Yep," said Coach Joe, scratching his chin. "What you're talking about is called process."

"Process? What process?"

"Some coaches will tell you that the process is more important than the results," said Coach Joe.

"I don't even know what that means," said Luis.

"It sounds weird, but just listen," said Coach Joe. "There are some coaches out there who say you shouldn't pay attention to whether or not you win or lose. What you should pay attention to is the process—the way you practice and do everything in between games.

"If you do that, they say, the winning will

take care of itself."

"Process…" said Luis, trying to understand.

"That's right," said Coach Joe. "And if you think about it, it makes sense. If you practice hard every time, then it becomes a habit. And then you automatically play hard in games, without even thinking about it.

"And if you play hard every game, you're probably going to win more than you lose."

"Sure," said Luis. "As long as you have good players."

"Haha," said Coach Joe. "That's true, Luis. That's absolutely true.

"What those coaches would say is that you can't focus on the results of your last game. If you start thinking too much about, say, winning 10-0, then you change your process. And if you change your process, it's only a matter of time until that causes you to stop winning."

"Process…" repeated Luis.

"Here's the deal," said Coach Joe. "You said before you wanted to have fun. And I agreed with you. But now you need to figure out a way to convince your teammates that they can't have *too* much fun."

"Why can't you do that?" asked Luis.

"I could try," said Coach Joe. "But it won't mean the same coming from me. It needs to come from you. You're the captain. You're not some grumpy old coach. You're one of the players."

"Well, what do I do?" asked Luis.

"That's what you have to decide," said Coach Joe.

Several days later, back at the Community baseball field, practice was about to start. It would be their third practice since they won 10–0, and their last practice before their next game.

It was their last chance to fix their process, Luis thought.

"Do you know why we always say, 'eyes up'?" asked Coach Joe.

"Because you want us to always be ready," Luis said. "To always look out for the ball."

"That's one reason, yes," said Coach Joe. "But there's another reason."

"Oh, what is that?" said Luis.

Coach Joe didn't say anything at first.

"I want you to think about it," he finally said. "Then tell me when you figure it out."

Luis and Coach Joe sat in silence for a few minutes.

"These coaches who talk about process," said Luis. "Are they good coaches?"

"Some of them are," said Coach Joe.

It was about halfway through practice when Luis lost his patience.

Aliyah and Gary were friends. He knew this, and he thought it was great. Sometimes, they seemed to be the only people on the team who were truly friends outside of baseball.

But a team captain can only take so many jokes and giggles in one practice. Enough was enough.

Aliyah was batting, Gary was catching, and Lisa was pitching, but Aliyah and Gary seemed to be only halfway paying attention. Aliyah would turn to Gary and whisper some kind of joke. Gary would burst into laughter. Lisa would throw a pitch. And then maybe Aliyah would swing at it, or maybe she wouldn't. And maybe Gary would catch it, or maybe he wouldn't.

Then they'd do it again.

It must have been a really funny joke, because they would not. Stop. Laughing.

"OK you know what?" Luis yelled out from his shortstop position. "Aliyah! Gary! That's it! Enough jokes! I'm sick of it! I'm glad you guys are having fun, but this is the last practice before our next game! We need to focus on getting better at baseball, not making each other laugh! And that goes for all of you out here. There is too much laughing and giggling and joking around, and not enough hustling and focusing and running after the ball!"

"Dude, relax," said Gary. "We won our last game 10–0."

It looked like Luis had actually hurt Gary's feelings, and Luis felt bad about that, but not bad enough to let it go.

"I don't care about our last game!" said Luis. "I care about our *next* game! And the way we've been practicing, we definitely aren't going to win the next one 10–0!"

"Yeah, we'll probably win 12–0," said Jimmie, watching all this happen from his spot at first base.

Everyone laughed. Aliyah and Gary did a fist

bump.

"Argh!" Luis yelled in frustration. He looked over at Coach Joe, who was watching from the dugout. Coach Joe took a step toward the field, then stopped and looked at Luis as if to say, "Do you want me to help?"

Luis shook his head in frustration.

"OK, look everybody," said Luis. "After practice today, we're going to have a team meeting."

"A team meeting?" said Jimmie, sounding grumpy.

Jimmie looked at Coach Joe for help.

"Players only!" said Luis. "And we're going to talk about the things we need to do to keep winning."

"Wait, a players-only team meeting?" asked Jimmie. "After our regular practice? No way, dude. I've got stuff to do."

"Stuff to do!" said Luis.

As he said this, Luis realized this was the first actual conversation that he and Jimmie had ever had.

It wasn't going well.

"What do you have to do?" said Luis.

"Well... uhm... just, stuff, OK?" said Jimmie as he kicked the ground.

"Listen," said Coach Joe, who had walked out onto the field without Luis even noticing. "I have to say something here. Luis is allowed to call a meeting after practice, but he's not allowed to make it required, OK? And neither am I. Practice ends in 45 minutes. After that, you're all free to go home. League rules.

"However... if you want to stay after for Luis's *optional* team meeting you can. No one will stop that from happening. Does everyone understand?"

"Basically, you're saying we don't have to go to Luis's dumb team meeting, is that right?" begged Jimmie.

"Well, except for the 'dumb' part, yes," said Coach Joe. "That's what I'm saying. I think a players-only team meeting is a good idea. But it's optional. Definitely optional.

"Sorry, Luis."

"It's fine, it's cool," said Luis. But he was a little bit disappointed that he couldn't require everyone to come to the meeting.

"Players-only team meeting after practice. Optional," he said. "Now let's get back to work."

The rest of practice was kind of better, but not really.

With just a few minutes left in practice, Coach Joe walked over to where Luis was fielding ground balls.

"The old players-only meeting, huh?" he half-whispered while looking like he was correcting Luis's footwork. "Let me know how it goes, OK?"

Luis half-whispered back, "Do team meetings ever work?"

Coach Joe stretched his hands over his head, scratched his chin and made a face that looked like he was thinking hard.

"Maybe... sometimes?"

"Great."

When practice ended, Coach Joe gave the team some final tips for their game the next day, then he turned them loose. Luis walked over to the side of the field.

"Team meeting over here!" he said. "Totally optional, of course!"

Only one player stuck around for the meeting, and it was Gary.

Obviously, Luis thought to himself, he had a lot more work to do to build a solid team.

CHAPTER 6

The "team meeting" of two got started as Luis and Gary sat together on the ground near home plate.

"I'm sorry I was joking around in practice too much," said Gary.

It really was impossible for Luis to stay mad when Gary was so polite.

"It's fine," said Luis. "I want everyone to have fun, I just...."

He wasn't sure exactly how to say what he wanted to say without coming across like the meanest teacher in school.

"I get it," said Gary. "As soon as you said something, I knew you were right."

Gary and Luis sat in silence for what seemed

like forever.

"Aliyah and I have been friends for a long time," said Gary. "We basically grew up together. There are pictures of us as babies just hanging out in some kind of playpen or something. I'm not sure if I actually remember doing that, or if I just remember looking at the pictures.

"But what I'm saying is, we're like brother and sister, except we don't fight as often as real brothers and sisters do."

"I get it," said Luis.

"Once we start laughing and joking, it's hard to stop."

"Hey, it's not a problem. But maybe every once in a while, you could just ease back on that a little bit. Stay cool. Help me keep everyone in line.

"That's my job, as team captain. Coach Joe says I'm supposed to make sure everybody has fun but also tries hard. It kind of seems impossible, so I could use your help."

"Yeah. Sure. I can do that," said Gary.

Then they sat around for a while again

without saying anything. Gary had a baseball in his right hand. Every once in a while he would toss it into his glove on his left hand. Then he'd take it out. Then he'd toss it back into his glove...

"Should we practice our throws for a little while?" said Luis. "I don't want to keep you here too long if you need to get home."

"That sounds good," said Gary. "I've got some time."

Gary and Luis tossed the baseball back and forth for 10 minutes or so without saying anything. But it wasn't weird. It was actually kind of fun.

"Hey," said Luis. "Do you want to work on your throws to second base? I know you said you haven't thrown anyone out trying to steal in... a while."

Gary laughed.

"It's OK. You can say it. I haven't thrown anybody out... ever!"

Luis laughed, too.

"I didn't want to say it like *that*," Luis said. "I mean, it's only, like, your biggest job!"

Now they were both laughing.

"I'll stand at second base," said Luis. "You set up behind home plate. Let's see if we can get better at this."

As they got to their positions, Gary said, "You know, a lot of people think throwing out runners is the catcher's only job. But that's not really true."

"Oh reaaaaaally," said Luis with a giggle.

"Haha," said Gary. "Yes, really. Did you know that some parent out there records every game in our league and puts it on the internet?"

"No," said Luis. "Really? Is that true?"

"Yep, it's true," said Gary. "Before every game we play, my dad and I watch the recordings of whoever we're about to play next. That way I get an idea of how good the players are. You know, how they like to hit the ball, stuff like that."

"You do that? Really?"

"Yeah, it's fun," said Gary. "That way, when we play them, I let Lisa know how she should pitch to certain batters. Like, maybe I'll see a guy hit a home run on a pitch that's outside. When they bat against us, I set up a little bit inside so when Lisa pitches, the ball goes inside a little bit.

"I'm not even sure if she realizes it. But I think it helps."

"I'm sure it does. That's really cool, Gary."

"Yeah, see? I told you! A catcher has to do more than just throw out runners."

"You're 100% right. But still, let's see if we can throw somebody out this year, OK? Now, eyes up!"

Gary laughed, and they practiced throwing for about 20 minutes before they both got tired.

When they were done, Luis really did think that Gary was getting better.

The Manatees lost their next game 6–4.

This team was much better than the first team they played, but still, Luis wasn't so sure that they were really any better than the Manatees.

Lisa didn't pitch as great as she normally did, and Coach Joe let Anthony pitch a few innings to give Lisa a break. That went about like it normally did—not great.

Luis played okay at shortstop, but he missed a ground ball that allowed a run to score. Roberto, normally really good, didn't get a single hit. Gary didn't throw anybody out trying to steal. Jimmie struck out three times before hitting a massive home run in the last inning. But it wasn't enough.

When it was over, Coach Joe gathered the team around him. He looked like he was about to say something, but then he stopped and looked at Luis.

"Luis? What did you think about the game today?"

Luis thought for a second.

"Well, we did some good things," he said, trying to watch his words very carefully. "But we also made a lot of mistakes."

"Are you talking about me, captain?" said Jimmie, and he said "captain" in that real sarcastic way that he had of saying things when he really wasn't happy. "Because if it wasn't for my home run, that game would have been even worse!"

This was the second conversation Jimmie and Luis had ever had, and it wasn't going any better than the first.

"I'm not talking about any single player," said Luis. "I'm talking about the team overall."

Jimmie quieted down, and nobody else really knew what to say.

"I agree with Luis," said Coach Joe. "Losing one game isn't the end of the world, but still, we can do a lot better than we did today. I'll see you guys at our next practice."

Nobody hung out too long after this game.

After a win, there are snacks and people laughing and telling jokes. Everyone is in a good mood, parents included. After a loss, there are still snacks, but they don't taste as good. Anyone who tries to make a joke… well, it just isn't really that funny.

As the players began walking to the parking lot with their parents, Luis found Gary.

"Hey Gary," said Luis. "You almost threw that one player out, today. She was just too fast. Nothing you could do about it. I think you're getting better."

"Thanks, captain," said Gary, and Luis could tell he appreciated it.

"Hey… so…" said Luis. "I'm thinking about calling another players-only meeting. Or players-only practice. Or… whatever. You know, to try to get everybody to practice harder, but still have fun, of course."

He kind of rolled his eyes at that last part, and Gary laughed.

"What do you think?" asked Luis.

"Well," said Gary as he lifted his bag of gear

over his shoulder. "I think that's fine, but it's not gonna do the team much good if you and me are the only people who show up to these things."

"Yep, that's true," said Luis.

"We need to get more people," said Gary. "We need to get the entire team in on this. Or else things are never going to get better."

"How do we do that?" asked Luis.

"Well," said Gary, taking a second to think about it. "Let's start with my best friend. If I can't get her to do it, then we're in big trouble."

CHAPTER 7

Aliyah's house wasn't very far from Luis's house. Gary and Luis were able to walk there in about 10 minutes.

Gary had been to Aliyah's house many times, so he gave Luis some scoop.

"She lives here with her mom and stepdad," said Gary. "They're both really nice, actually. She's lucky."

Luis nodded.

"Her stepdad is really big on being polite and respectful," Gary continued. "Look him straight in the eye, shake his hand, all that stuff."

"Got it," said Luis.

"It's going to be fine," said Gary.

And only then did Luis start to get nervous

thinking he would surely make a mistake.

"Why wouldn't it be fine?" said Luis.

"Oh, no reason," said Gary.

That only made Luis more nervous.

"You look nervous. You're fidgeting," said Gary. "Stop doing that."

"Stop doing what?"

"Looking nervous. Just chill out. Be cool."

"Well, you're making me nervous!"

"How am I making you nervous? I told you it was going to be fine!"

"But why did you say that in the first place? I mean, why *wouldn't* it be fine?"

"I said it because it's true!" said Gary. "It's going to be fine!"

"Oh boy," said Luis.

They were at the front door. Gary lifted his hand to knock on the door, but it opened before he had the chance.

"Gary!" said two people at the same time.

One was a tall, nice-looking woman that Luis figured was Aliyah's mom. The other was a giant man that Luis figured was her stepdad.

"Your mom told me you were on your way," Aliyah's mom said to Gary. "How you doing big man?"

She leaned over and gave Gary a hug.

"How you doing, Gare?" said Aliyah's stepdad.

"I'm doing great," said Gary. "How are you guys?"

"We're doing just fine, sweetheart," said Aliyah's mom.

And only then did Aliyah's parents turn and look at Luis.

"Hello," said Luis, as politely as he could.

"Hello there," said Aliyah's mom, and Luis kind of felt like she was trying her best to be polite and not say what she really wanted to say.

Aliyah's stepdad didn't say anything.

"This is Luis," said Gary. "From the Manatees. He's our —"

"Uh-huh," said Aliyah's mom. "I know who this is. It's nice to meet you, Luis."

"It's nice to meet you, too," said Luis. He stuck out his hand to shake with Aliyah's stepdad, and the giant man reluctantly shook back.

And then they all four just stood there.

"So, uhm, we're here to talk to Aliyah about some quick baseball stuff... it won't take long," said Gary.

Aliyah's mom looked back to Gary and immediately seemed much more warm and friendly.

"Of course, Gary," she said. "You're welcome here anytime. You know that."

She looked at Luis but didn't say anything. Aliyah's stepdad just stood there.

"Thank you," said Gary. "Right. So. Uhm... we'll just go talk to Aliyah then."

He looked at Luis and motioned him to follow him into the house.

Luis started to walk forward, but he wasn't sure if Aliyah's parents were going to move out of the way.

They did, just in time.

"You want anything to eat or drink, Gary?" Aliyah's mom asked as the boys entered the house and headed toward what Luis guessed would be

Aliyah's room.

"No thank you, we're good," said Gary.

Luis whispered to Gary, "Actually I wouldn't mind having—"

"Nope, you're good," said Gary.

"Oh. OK. Exactly. I'm good," said Luis.

They turned to the left and walked down a hallway. Gary knew exactly where to go.

"What is going on?" said Luis, and he managed to say it in a whisper but also very loud at the same time."

"Shhh!" whispered Gary. "You're fine. It's fine."

"It doesn't seem fine," said Luis.

They came to a closed door at the end of the hall. Gary knocked.

"Hey Aliyah. It's me," said Gary.

"And me, too," said Luis.

Gary looked at Luis and shook his head furiously, right as Aliyah opened the door.

"Hey!" said Gary.

"Uh-huh," said Aliyah, looking at Luis.

"Hi Aliyah," said Luis. "We just want to talk

about the Manatees."

Aliyah looked at Gary. He shrugged his shoulders.

"Well, it better be quick," said Aliyah. "I've got homework."

Aliyah's room was full of baseball stuff.

In one corner sat a bat and glove that looked like they'd be too small for Aliyah to use these days. Luis figured they must have been from when she was little.

On one shelf sat some signed pictures and cards from her favorite players. Luis noticed they were all outfielders, and they were all known for their speed.

And one shelf was full of trophies.

There were a lot of trophies.

"Wow," said Luis. "You've been on a lot of winning teams it looks like."

"Yes, I have," said Aliyah.

No one said anything for a minute.

It was kind of awkward. Gary and Aliyah sat next to each other on the edge of her bed as Luis was left standing alone.

"Uhm, Aliyah?" said Luis. "I felt like things were kind of weird when I met your mom and stepdad out there. Do you know anything about that?"

"Oh, I just told them that you stole my job as captain and that I'll always hate you for it, that's all," said Aliyah.

"Wait!" said Luis. "For real? Why would you say that?"

"Because it's true!" said Aliyah. "I should have been captain."

"What?" said Luis again.

"Guys let's just take it easy, OK?" said Gary.

"I should have been captain," repeated Aliyah. "I've been with the Manatees longer than you. I've helped them win tons of games. And somehow, you're the team captain and not me."

"OK," said Gary. "Listen guys…"

"Hey, I didn't want to be captain," said Luis. "Coach Joe just chose me for no reason!"

"He chose you because you came up with that ridiculous answer to that ridiculous question!" said Aliyah.

"Guys," said Gary.

"I had no idea how I was supposed to answer that question!" said Luis.

"That's not true," said Aliyah. "You just said what you thought Coach Joe wanted to hear because you were just *dying* to be captain even though you're new here."

"I did not!" said Luis. "I answered honestly, and it just happened to be what Coach Joe wanted to hear!"

"Guys!" said Gary, and he didn't exactly yell,

but he said it loud enough to get their attention.

"Listen," continued Gary. "Aliyah, I don't think you're being fair. Luis didn't want to be captain, but Coach Joe made him captain anyway, and now he's just doing the best he can."

"Yes, thank you Gary," said Luis.

"And Luis," said Gary. "Think about how Aliyah feels. Imagine if you were with the same team for a long time, and you wanted to be captain, but your coach gave it to someone else?"

"Right, thanks Gary," said Aliyah.

"We're all on the same team here," said Gary. "Like, for real. We're all on the same team—the Manatees. We need to work this out."

"Fine," said Aliyah.

"Fine," echoed Luis.

But nobody said anything for quite some time.

Finally, Luis spoke up to break the silence.

"Listen, Aliyah," he said. "I'm sorry. I didn't know you wanted to be captain. I don't know what else I can do though. Coach Joe named me captain, and now I'm captain."

Aliyah didn't say anything at first. But then she looked at Gary, and he looked back at her like, "Well?"

"Fine," said Aliyah. "I'm over it."

Luis didn't think she was really over it, but at least they were making progress.

"Aliyah," said Luis. "My goal is the same as your goal. I want the Manatees to play better. We didn't play well in our last game, and we haven't been doing great at practice, either.

"I think after we won that first game 10–0, we got kind of relaxed or something. Now I want us to try to get back to what we were doing before, when we were having fun but also working hard.

"I think we should start getting together after practice—players only. We can talk about what's going on, maybe get some extra practice in. Or whatever we feel like doing. It would mean a lot to me if you'd be there Aliyah."

Aliyah looked at Luis, then at Gary, and let out a big sigh.

"You're on board with this?" she asked Gary.

"Yeah, I am," said Gary. "I think it's a good idea."

"Even though he's captain when obviously I should be captain," said Aliyah.

"I know," said Gary. "That part stinks."

"Uhm, guys?" said Luis. "I'm standing right here."

"He's a nice guy," said Gary. "Just look at him. Standing there all pitiful. Don't you feel sorry for him?"

"OK," said Luis. "Not funny."

"He is kind of pitiful," said Aliyah. "I'm just not sure about the nice guy part."

"Again, I'm right here, guys," said Luis. "Standing right here. Hearing every word you're saying."

"Let's give him a chance," said Gary. "Have I ever steered you wrong?"

"Yes, many times," said Aliyah.

"That's correct," Gary said. "I have. Many times."

They all three laughed.

"But if you say we should do this, Gary, then fine, I'll do it," said Aliyah.

"Yes!" said Luis excitedly. "This is great. You won't regret it. I promise."

"Sure," said Aliyah, "we'll see about that. Who else has agreed to come to these team meetings, by the way?"

"Just the three of us, so far," said Luis. "But I hope to get everyone there eventually."

"How are you going to do that?" asked Aliyah.

"By begging, basically," said Luis.

Aliyah laughed at that.

"Hey, it worked on you!" said Luis. "Who should we ask next?"

Gary and Aliyah looked at each other.

"You thinking what I'm thinking?" Aliyah said to Gary.

"I'm afraid so, yes," Gary answered.

Then they both said it at the same time: "Roberto."

★ CHAPTER 8 ★

The Manatees lost their next game, 3–2.

But they played a lot better, playing more as a team than in game 2.

The problem was, this time their opponent was a really good team. Their pitcher threw super fast, almost as fast as Lisa. The Manatees hit a lot of balls really hard, but the other team had good fielders. They caught it almost every time.

Roberto had three hits, but it wasn't enough.

"We played a lot better today, guys," Coach Joe told the team after the game. "I'm proud of how we played. But we still have room to get better. Luis? Anything you want to say?"

Luis felt like he was starting to get the hang of this.

"That was a good team we played against," said Luis. "And I agree with Coach Joe that we did play better. But…"

"Here we go," said Jimmie. "There's always something with this guy."

"We're good enough to beat teams like this. We just have to start trying harder in practice," said Luis.

"What are you going to do?" asked Jimmie. "Have another team meeting? After basically nobody showed up to the last one?"

"Yes," said Luis. "That's exactly what I'm going to do. We're going to have another team meeting."

He looked at Coach Joe.

"Optional, of course," Luis said.

"It looks like Roberto's in a good mood," Luis said to Gary and Aliyah as Roberto was high-fiving some of the team. The three of them were standing together, trying to look casual. "Maybe now's a good time to talk to him?"

Gary and Luis looked at Aliyah.

"Sure," she said. "Let's do this. But Luis, you have to talk first. He'll never listen to me."

"OK, fine," said Luis.

They saw Roberto walking toward the parking lot with his parents. Luis ran to catch up.

"Hey! Roberto!" he said.

Roberto turned around, and his parents did, too.

"Hi guys," said Luis. "I'm Luis. Sorry to bother you. Do you mind if I just talk to Roberto for a second about some baseball stuff? It'll just take a few minutes."

"I don't have time," said Roberto.

"Oh Bert," said his mom. "Go talk to your friend."

Then to Luis, "It's fine, honey. Take your time!"

"Mom!" said Roberto. "He's not my friend!"

"Just go talk to him son," said Roberto's dad. "It's fine. We'll wait."

"Ugh," Roberto sighed as if he'd been asked

to do something impossible, like swim across the ocean or something.

"Thank you!" said Luis. "It'll only be a minute!"

Luis led Roberto to the other side of the snack stand, where Aliyah and Gary were waiting.

"What is *she* doing here?" said Roberto, pointing at Aliyah.

"Just wait a second," said Luis. "Don't walk away. Let's talk through this."

"I've got nothing to say," said Roberto. "Except she stole my spot in center field! I should be the center fielder!"

"Hey," said Aliyah. "It's not my fault I'm a better center fielder than you!"

"What!" said Roberto. "I was doing fine in center field until I came to the Manatees!"

"Well, guess what?" said Aliyah. "Now you're the second-best center fielder on the team. Congratulations."

"How do you think it's going so far?" Gary whispered to Luis.

"Ugh," was all Luis could think to say.

"You know what?" said Roberto. "I don't need this. I'm going home."

"Wait," said Luis. "Roberto, just wait a second. Let's talk this out."

Roberto stopped and looked at Luis. Then he looked at Gary.

"You've got two minutes," Roberto said.

"OK. Great. Thank you. Listen," said Luis. "You played great today. You really did. But you know the team hasn't played as good as we can the last couple of weeks. It wouldn't be a big deal; except everyone knows we can do better. Right?"

Roberto didn't say anything.

"The three of us all think we can do better," said Gary. "What we need to do is really come together as a team. Work hard. Have fun. We can do it, but it only works if everybody buys in."

Roberto looked at the two of them, then at Aliyah.

"Aliyah," said Luis. "Think about how you felt when I was named captain. Now think about how Roberto might have felt when you were named starting center fielder. Do you see how maybe it might be kind of the same thing?"

Aliyah's eyes widened.

She looked at Roberto, and Roberto looked at the ground.

"I think it's working," whispered Gary to Luis.

"Shhh!" Luis whispered back.

"Roberto," said Luis. "The reason I'm calling

these players-only meetings... or practices... or whatever, is because I think it will help us be a better team. And you're one of our best players. It would be awesome if you could make it to the next one. What do you say?"

Roberto didn't say anything. He was thinking about it.

"Sorry," said Aliyah.

That took all three boys by surprise.

"What?" said Roberto.

"I'm sorry if I came across as mean to you," said Aliyah. "I didn't mean to. I can totally understand if you were upset at me getting to play center field. I would have felt the same way if it had been switched."

"OK," said Roberto.

"But here's the deal," said Aliyah. "Coach Joe does what he thinks is best for the team. And that means me playing center field. And it also means this guy being team captain and calling these dumb team meetings."

Roberto and Aliyah laughed.

"Didn't see that coming," Gary whispered to

Luis.

"Shhh!" whispered Luis.

"I'm going to be there," said Aliyah. "Will you come too, Roberto?"

Roberto looked at Luis, then Gary, then Aliyah.

"Fine," he said.

"Yes!" said Luis, Gary and Aliyah, fist-bumping all at the same time.

"This is great," said Luis. "It's going to be worth it; I promise. The more people we can get to come to these meetings, the better we're going to do as a team."

"How many people are in so far?" asked Roberto.

"Just the four of us for now," said Gary.

"Huh," said Roberto.

He thought for a second.

"Well, I'm friends with several players on the Manatees who played on my school team last year," said Roberto. "If I tell them to come, they'll come."

"Wow," said Luis. "You'd do that? That would

be great."

"You really think it'll make us a better team?" asked Roberto.

"I do," said Luis. "I think it'll make us a better team, and it'll make baseball more fun for all of us."

Roberto nodded his head.

"Fine," he said. "I'll be there. And I'll bring my friends, too."

"Yes!" said Gary, pumping his fist in the air.

"You won't regret this, Bert-man," said Luis.

Everyone froze. Luis meant it as a joke, but it didn't look like Roberto took it that way.

"S-sorry," stuttered Luis. "It's just that... I heard your mom call you Bert-man.... I thought it was a cool nickname.... I didn't mean to..."

Roberto walked right up to Luis and looked him straight in the eye.

"It is a cool nickname," Roberto said.

"Yeah," said Luis. "Totally."

They both looked at each other.

"I'll see you at the meeting," said Roberto, and he jogged off to catch up to his parents.

★ CHAPTER 9 ★

The next person they convinced to come to the meeting was Lisa, but it turned out to be easy. Gary walked up to her before practice, asked her if she wouldn't mind coming, and she said, "Sure, no problem." ·

When you counted all of Roberto's friends, Luis figured about half of his teammates were on board. The other half might need more convincing.

Practice, in the meantime, was just OK. They did some things good. They did some things not so good. Coach Joe was happy sometimes. The rest of the time, he wasn't. For the most part, Luis agreed with him. They were getting better, but they still weren't as good as they could be if they could just get everybody on the same page.

When practice was over, Luis reminded everyone of the players-only meeting that would follow.

"Boring!" said Jimmie. Some of the players laughed, but not all of them.

"So, what do we do at these meetings?" asked Lisa.

Practice had ended, and, just as Luis expected, about half the players stuck around.

But now, no one knew what do, including Luis.

"Well… ," said Luis. Then he looked at Gary.

"Well, we just…" said Gary, who looked at Aliyah.

"Oh brother, you guys are lame," said Aliyah. "What we're *supposed* to do is, we talk about baseball, and maybe practice a few things if we want to. But this is the first time anyone other than Gary and Luis have come to one of these meetings, so who knows."

"I gotcha," said Lisa. "That's cool."

"Cool, thanks Aliyah" said Luis.

"Yeah, cool," said Gary.

Roberto and his friends were tossing a baseball around the outfield. Lisa, Gary, Aliyah and Luis were just kind of standing there.

"Hey Gary," said Luis. "Why don't you set up behind the plate. Lisa, you throw him some practice pitches. And Gary, you throw the ball down to second base, like you're trying to catch a base stealer."

"Good idea," said Gary.

"Yeah, good idea," said Lisa.

"What should I do?" asked Aliyah.

"Well," said Luis. "Maybe go practice with Roberto?"

"Seriously?" whispered Aliyah.

"Yes, seriously," said Luis. "Go out there and be friendly. He's a great player and I'm sure he's a nice person. It's time for us to all start playing like a real team. Eyes up, Aliyah. You've got this."

"Fine," said Aliyah.

Lisa wound up and threw a practice pitch to Gary. Even though she wasn't throwing as hard as she could, it was still plenty hard.

The ball made a loud *thwack!* sound when it hit Gary's glove. Then Gary hopped up and threw the ball to second. Luis caught it and practiced tagging out a runner who was trying to steal.

"Not bad, Gary," said Luis.

"Seriously," said Lisa. "Not bad at all. You been practicing this, Gary?"

"Well, kind of, yeah," said Gary, feeling proud.

Luis, Lisa and Gary kept practicing for around 30 minutes. They laughed and they joked around, but they never stopped working hard. It was just like Luis thought it should be.

Every once in a while, Luis would look out into the outfield, and he'd see Aliyah and Roberto and Roberto's friends tossing the ball around. Was it Luis's imagination, or were they laughing and joking and getting along just fine? Maybe being team captain isn't so bad after all he thought to himself.

Before everyone went home, Luis asked his teammates to gather around him, just like Coach Joe would do after a practice.

"So, what did you guys think about our meeting?" Luis asked.

The players looked at each other.

"Not bad," said Lisa.

"Yeah, not bad," said Roberto.

"OK," said Luis. "Good job everybody. I'll see you at practice tomorrow."

"That's it?" said Roberto. "We're done?"

"That's it," said Luis. "We're done."

"Well, what was the point of all this?" said Roberto. "What did I stick around for?"

"Did you have fun?" asked Luis.

"Yeah, I did," Roberto admitted.

"Well," said Luis. "That was the point."

Luis was walking off the practice field with Aliyah and Gary after their meeting when Gary suddenly stopped.

"What is it?" said Luis.

"Luis," said Gary. "There's one more thing you need to do, and I think you know what it is."

"What?" said Luis. "What are you talking about?"

"He's right," said Aliyah. "Luis, it's time."

"Time for what?" Luis asked.

Gary and Aliyah said it at the same time: "You need to talk to Jimmie."

The Manatees won their next game 6–4. Then they lost the game after that. Then they won a couple of games in a row. Then they lost one. Then they won a few more.

And so it went, until the season was almost over.

The Manatees were good. They were winning more often than they were losing.

And still, Luis had not talked to Jimmie.

"How are your team meetings going?" Coach Joe asked Luis after one practice.

"Good," said Luis. "Real good, actually. It's fun to get together with my teammates and just kind of relax. You know, maybe practice baseball a little bit, but also just hang out and talk about other stuff."

"That's great," said Coach Joe. "You're a true team captain now. Good job, Luis."

"Well," said Luis. "Not quite."

"What do you mean?" asked Coach Joe.

"There's still one thing I need to do, that I just haven't quite gotten around to doing yet," said Luis.

"Oh," said Coach Joe. "Well, do you want to talk about it?"

"So, what happens is, only about half the team shows up to our meetings," said Luis.

"OK, well, that's not too bad," said Coach Joe.

"Yeah, I know," said Luis. "It's just that…"
Luis hesitated.

"The other half is Jimmie and his friends, right?" said Coach Joe.

"Yep," said Luis. "That's exactly right."

"OK," said Coach Joe. "So, what are you going to do?"

"I don't know," said Luis. "What do you think I should do?"

Coach Joe scratched his chin that way that he did when he was thinking about something real hard.

"I think you have two choices," he said finally. "You can keep doing what you're doing. The team is doing pretty good. Practices have been better. Not always great, but better. The team seems to be playing fine. Maybe not as a good as we could play. But still fine. If you just keep doing what you're doing, things will probably be okay. Or... you can talk to Jimmie."

"Right," said Luis.

For a minute, neither of them said anything.

"I guess I know what I have to do," said Luis finally.

"Hey Gary, Lisa, Roberto, Aliyah," Luis said to his friends after practice. "No team meeting after practice today. Spread the word.

"I'm going to talk to Jimmie."

Gary, Lisa, Roberto and Aliyah looked at

each other.

"Wow," said Roberto.

"Yeah, wow," said Lisa.

"Good luck," said Gary and Aliyah.

Luis decided he would treat this like pulling a bandage off a scrape. It's better to do it quickly and get it over with than to do it slowly and make it last longer.

So, he walked right up to Jimmie as soon as practice was over.

"Hey Jimmie," he said.

"Oh boy," said Jimmie. "What… no players-only meeting today?"

"No," said Luis. "But I'd like to talk to you, if that's OK."

Luis and Jimmie had only had a few conversations, and none of them had gone well. Luis was determined that this time, it'd be different.

"Well, captain," Jimmie said with that sarcastic voice of his. "I'm really busy today. Lots of things to do, you know."

"Yeah, I know," said Luis. "It won't take long."

Jimmie let out a deep breath.

"Fine," he said. "What do you want?"

Then it was Luis's turn to take a deep breath. This was his chance—maybe his only chance—to get Jimmie on his side. If he messed this up, he might never get another chance, and the Manatees would never be as good of a team as they could be.

He figured his best bet was to just come out and say it.

"You haven't been coming to our team meetings," he said.

"Yeah," said Jimmie. "So what? You said they were optional."

"Yeah, that's true," said Luis. "They are. But most of the players try to come at least every once in a while. That's all I've ever asked."

"None of my friends have gone," said Jimmie.

"Yes, exactly," said Luis. "Do you think, maybe, you could ask them to come? Just, you know, a few times? Every once in a while?"

"Why would I do that?" asked Jimmie.

"Because I really think that these meetings

help make us a better team," said Luis. "We talk about baseball. We talk about school and other things. We joke around. We maybe practice a little bit, but mostly we just hang out and become... well... friends."

"Haha," laughed Jimmie. "You think you and I could be... well... friends?"

He was using the sarcastic voice again.

"We don't have to be friends," said Luis. "But we could be better... teammates, maybe."

Jimmie stood there for a second and thought about it.

"I tell you what," he said finally. "I'll come to your silly meetings, and I'll bring my friends with me, if..."

"Oh gosh," thought Luis. "What is *this* going to be about?"

"If..." continued Jimmie. "You can hit a home run. Right here. Right now."

What?" said Luis. "A home run? Jimmie, I'm not really that kind of hitter. I can hit singles and doubles and triples... but not home runs."

"Why not?" asked Jimmie. "What's stopping you?"

"Well," Luis said. He was going to have to admit something that he didn't want to admit. "I'm not as strong as, like, you are. I'm fast. But I'm not that strong. So, I can't hit the ball over the fence. But I can hit it in between the outfielders, and then run as fast as I can."

"Phhhh," said Jimmie. "Hitting home runs isn't all about being strong, dude."

"Easy for you to say!" said Luis. "You're... strong!"

Jimmie laughed.

"Fair enough," said Jimmie. "But listen. Here's the deal. If you can hit a home run right here, right now, me and my friends will come to your next meeting. If not... no deal."

"What?" Luis said for the second time. "But I can't even... who's even going to pitch to me?"

Luis looked around. Everyone had either left or was on their way out.

"I'll pitch to you," said Jimmie, picking up a bag full of baseballs. "There's probably about 25 baseballs in this bag. That means you've got 25 chances to hit a home run.

"Don't worry. I won't throw it too hard."

Then Jimmie winked at Luis.

Luis began to think that Jimmie was having a little too much fun with this.

"Have you ever even pitched before?" asked Luis.

"Sure! Lots of times," said Jimmie. "I'm not that bad at it, if we're being honest here."

Jimmie walked out to the pitcher's mound with the bag of baseballs, but Luis just stood there.

"Jimmie," said Luis. "This isn't fair!"

"Oh, quit your whining," said Jimmie. "Just get up there and hit a home run. Eyes up, Luis!"

CHAPTER 11

Woosh!

The first pitch that Jimmie threw to Luis zoomed right over the plate. With no catcher there to catch it, it clanged against the fence about 15 feet behind where the catcher would normally be.

It wasn't a bad pitch, actually.

"Why didn't you swing at that?" asked Jimmie.

Luis didn't really have an answer for him.

"Just… give me a second," he said. "Have I said yet that I don't really hit home runs?"

Jimmie chuckled.

Again, Luis got the impression that Jimmie was enjoying this.

Luis put his bat on his shoulder. He'd be ready

for the next pitch.

But Jimmie didn't look like he was going to throw it just yet.

"When's the last time you hit a home run?" Jimmie asked.

"The last time I hit a home run?" Luis asked. He took the bat off his shoulder.

"Uhm… OK… well… to be honest… I've never hit a home run over the fence," Luis admitted.

"What? Really?" said Jimmie laughing.

"The last time I hit a home run was in a game where there were no fences," said Luis. "If you hit the ball between the outfielders, it would just roll and roll and roll and you could run forever. So that's how I hit my last home run."

"Oh wow," said Jimmie. "You really aren't very strong, are you?"

This time it was Luis who chuckled.

"You know what?" Luis said. "Fine. Just throw the pitch."

"Now we're talking!" said Jimmie, suddenly very excited. "That's the attitude I wanted to see!

Not some wimpy excuses."

Jimmie wound up and threw another pitch right over the plate. It was just the right speed for a home run hitter to smash a home run.

Luis was not a home run hitter and that was becoming clear. He smashed a ball into right field that would have been a double in a real game.

"OK," said Jimmie, nodding his head. "Not bad."

"I told you," said Luis. "I hit singles and doubles and triples. Not home runs."

"Yeah," said Jimmie. "I heard you the first time you said that."

In came another pitch. This time Luis ripped it to left. Probably a single in a real game.

The next pitch, Luis smashed a ground ball up the middle. Probably a base hit, unless the other team had a really good shortstop.

After a few more pitches, and a few more hits that definitely were not home runs, Luis called for a timeout.

"Give me a second to catch my breath," he said. "All these base hits are wearing me out."

"Haha," said Jimmie. "The deal wasn't base hits. The deal was a home run. Or I don't come to your silly meetings."

"I know, I know," said Luis.

Luis stood in the batter's box for a minute, shaking out his arms and catching his breath, getting ready to hit again.

Jimmie watched him from the pitcher's mound.

"You need to tighten up your swing," said Jimmie, out of nowhere. "Make it more compact."

"Say what?" said Luis.

"I said you need to tighten up your swing!" said Jimmie, but he said it loudly, pretending like Luis was having trouble hearing him.

Of course, Luis wasn't having trouble hearing him. He was having trouble understanding him.

"I don't know what that means," said Luis.

Jimmie walked from the pitcher's mound to the batter's box where Luis was standing.

"Here, give me the bat," said Jimmie. "Let me show you."

Luis gave him his bat.

"My mom played softball in college," said Jimmie.

"Really?" asked Luis.

"When I was little, she taught me how to swing a bat," said Jimmie. "That's why I can hit so many home runs.

"Yes, being the biggest kid my age helps. But that's not the only thing."

"Wow," said Luis. "That's cool. I had no idea—"

"Do you want me show you, or not?" said Jimmie.

"Yes," said Luis. "Yes, of course."

Jimmie took the bat and held it like he was about to swing. He held his hands out, away from his body, like Luis did.

"This is how you swing," said Jimmie. "With your hands way out like this."

Jimmie wiggled the bat back and forth.

"You need to bring your hands in closer to your body," said Jimmie.

Then he brought his hands in closer to his chest.

"When your hands are closer to your body, you can swing with a lot more power," said Jimmie. "When you swing like this..." (he moved his hands back out, away from his body) "... you're only swinging with your arms. But when you swing like this..." (he moved his hands back closer to his body) "… you can use the muscles in your chest and waist and your arms.

"It helps you swing harder."

"Wow," said Luis. "Thanks. That's really—"

"Not that you have that many muscles anyway," said Jimmie, but he smiled when he said it, and Luis smiled, too.

Luis didn't hit any home runs. But by taking Jimmie's advice, he was able to hit the ball harder than ever before. With enough practice, he figured he could probably hit one over the fence.

But there were only 25 or so baseballs in that bag, and it wasn't enough for Luis to get a homer.

The last pitch, Luis smacked the ball a long, long way. It banged off the bottom of the fence. So close, but probably another triple in a real game.

"Oooooh!" said Jimmie. "Almost! So close dude! Nice job!"

Jimmie walked closer to Luis, and it looked like he was going to give Luis a high-five. But

Luis was looking down at the ground.

"So, this means you won't come to our meetings?" asked Luis. "Is that right? After all this, you still won't come!"

"Ahh," Jimmie said. "I'll come to your dumb meetings."

"Really?" said Luis.

"Yes, of course I will," said Jimmie. "Why do you think I'm here right now? I was planning on coming to the meeting today, but you canceled it."

"What? You mean, you were already planning on coming to the meeting?" said Luis. "I thought you said you were busy!"

"I am busy after practice! But I asked my mom if I could start coming to at least a few of these meetings, and she said it was OK."

"But…" said Luis. "Then why… What was the point of this whole thing we just did?"

"I dunno," said Jimmie. "I thought it was kind of fun. Didn't you? And you're all about having fun."

"Well… actually… yeah, I guess it was," said Luis.

"When's the next meeting?" asked Jimmie.

"After practice tomorrow, I guess," said Luis.

"I'll be there," said Jimmie. "And I'll make sure my friends are there, too."

Jimmie gave Luis a fist bump.

"You know, you're a lot nicer person than I thought," said Luis.

"Yeah, I get that a lot," said Jimmie. "I'm not sure why people think I'm not nice."

"Hmmm," said Luis. "Maybe I can help you with that. You help me hit home runs; I'll help you be friendlier to people."

Jimmie looked at Luis like he wasn't sure. But then he smiled and said, "Deal."

★ CHAPTER 12 ★

The first team meeting with the entire team went great.

Gary worked some more on trying to throw out runners who were trying to steal. Lisa and Anthony threw some pitches for some of the players who wanted to practice their hitting. And even Jimmie had fun, chatting with his teammates and whacking a few home run balls over the fence.

And it came just in time, too. The Manatees' first playoff game was in three days.

The regular season had gone well. They won more games than they lost, which was good. They made the playoffs, which was even better. And now they were finally coming together as a team, which was great.

Nothing could stop them now!

Luis gathered his teammates around him.

"Hey Gary," said Luis. "I know you like to watch videos of other teams in our league to get an idea of how good they are. What can you tell us about the Tigers?"

"Yeah, I'm not going to lie to you guys," said Gary. "They're good."

He paused for a second and looked around at the rest of the team.

"But that doesn't mean we can't beat them."

"Got it," said Luis. "Tell us what we need to know."

Gary told them how the Tigers had a third baseman who could hit a lot of home runs. And they had a pitcher who could throw really hard. And they also had a center fielder who could catch anything. Oh and a catcher who could throw out any runner who was trying to steal bases.

"Wow," said Luis.

He looked around at his teammates. They all looked kind of worried.

"It sounds like they're really good," said Luis.

"Yes," said Gary. "But I noticed a few other things, too."

Gary told them he never saw the third baseman hit a home run on a pitch inside, only on pitches that were outside.

"OK," said Lisa. "Good to know. I'll only throw him pitches inside."

"Great," said Luis. "What else?"

Gary told them the pitcher who throws really hard doesn't always throw strikes.

"If you take enough pitches, he might walk you," Gary said.

"I don't like taking pitches, I like swinging at pitches. If you guys can't handle that, then you suck," said Jimmie.

Everyone looked at him.

Luis leaned over and whispered to him, "And you wonder why people think you aren't friendly?"

Jimmie rolled his eyes and grinned.

"But in this case, fine, I'll try to make him walk me," he said.

"Awesome," said Luis. "What else?"

Gary told them that the center fielder who was really fast likes to stand too close to the infield. That means it might be easy to get a ball over his head, even though he is really fast. And the catcher who could throw out any runner? Well, that catcher hadn't tried to throw out anyone as fast as Aliyah.

"You got that right," said Aliyah, and the rest of the Manatees patted her on the back and gave her high-fives.

"OK everybody, I have one last thing to say," said Luis. "The playoffs are tough. They're supposed to be tough. If we lose this game, our season is over. Only the best teams make the playoffs, so it totally makes sense that we'd be up against a really good team here, right? But listen…"

Everyone was quiet.

"We're the Manatees," he said. "We can do this. If we stick together as team, there's nothing we can't do!

"Eyes up, everybody!"

"Eyes up!" they all shouted at the same time.

And then everyone—Luis, Gary, Aliyah, Lisa, Roberto, Jimmie, and everybody else— cheered and patted each other on the back.

The Manatees lost their playoff game 5–2, and their season was over.

But it wasn't all bad!

Luis made a lot of good plays at shortstop. And thanks to the hitting advice Jimmie gave him, he even knocked a ball over the center fielder's head all the way to the outfield fence. Not quite a home run, but it was closer than he'd ever come before in a real game.

Lisa pitched really well. She just made one mistake to the Tigers' third baseman that resulted in them scoring three runs.

Jimmie hit a home run, of course, like he always did, and Aliyah, Roberto and everyone else made some great plays.

But the highlight of the game came in the seventh inning, when the Tigers had a runner on first base with two out. With two strikes on the batter, the runner tried to steal second. Gary caught the pitch from Lisa, stood up as fast as he could, and fired the ball to second base.

Luis was right there. He caught the throw from Gary and tagged the runner just as he slid into second base...

He was out! For the first time ever, Gary had thrown out a runner trying to steal.

Every single Manatee ran to Gary and either gave him a hug, gave him a high-five, or both. The Manatees were celebrating so much, the players on the other team probably thought they were confused about the score or something.

But they weren't. That's just how happy they were for their teammate. They felt like a true team now.

In the postgame handshake line, every member of the Tigers said, "Good game, Manatees," and every member of the Manatees said, "Good game, Tigers."

Later, Coach Joe asked everybody to gather around him one last time. It would be the last time they gathered around like this until next season.

"Well guys, I'm proud of you," he said. "We lost today, but sometimes that's what happens. If just a few plays had gone differently, we might have won. But that's OK. I'm proud of how hard we played."

Everyone clapped politely.

Then came his usual, "Luis? Do you have

anything to say?"

Now everyone clapped louder, and some even let out a cheer. Luis was almost embarrassed, but more proud than anything.

"Yeah, Luis!" said Roberto.

"Attaboy, captain!" said Jimmie.

"I... I don't really know what to say," said Luis. He was surprised at how sad he was that the season was over. He woke up this morning thinking they were going to win and get to play another game. But now, it was all over.

And they were all just starting to become friends!

It was true: For the first time since way back at the beginning of the season, Luis really didn't know what to say.

"Captain?" said Jimmie. "Can I say something?"

"Sure, Jimmie," said Luis. "Go ahead."

Luis was relieved that someone else was going to talk.

"I just want to say these last few days have been super fun," said Jimmie. "I've enjoyed playing baseball with all of you."

Then he turned to look at Luis.

"Even you, Luis."

Everyone laughed.

"Yeah, me too," said Gary. "This was a great season."

"Me too," said Aliyah.

Then everyone started saying "yeah!" And "me too!" And a few people said, "Go Manatees!"

"OK, OK," said Luis. "Settle down everybody. I get it. You all did great. I'm proud to be a Manatee. Eyes up, everybody. I'll see you next year!"

CHAPTER 13

It was a long, cold winter. It was made even worse by not having baseball and getting to be outside in the park every day.

But Gary, Aliyah and Luis spent a lot of time together anyway. They watched movies, helped each other with their homework, and helped each other out with anything else whenever anyone needed it.

Sometimes they just hung out and did nothing at all.

Sometimes they'd throw the baseball outside, but it wasn't the same when you had to wear a winter jacket and hat. Sometimes they'd throw the baseball inside the school gym, but it wasn't the same when you had to do it indoors.

Finally, one day in March, Luis knocked on Gary's door.

"Hey, Luis," said Gary.

"Hey, Gary," said Luis.

"What's going on?" said Gary.

"Well, I just checked the weather. This afternoon, for the first time this year, it's going to be warm enough to toss the baseball… outside… without having to wear a winter jacket."

"Is that right?" said Gary.

"Yep," said Luis. "That's right."

"You thinking what I'm thinking?" asked Gary.

"Whose house should we go to first?" asked Luis.

They split up.

Gary went to Aliyah's house. Luis went to Lisa's. Gary went to Roberto's. Luis went to Jimmie's.

"You're telling me you went and got Gary, Aliyah, Lisa and Roberto before you came to get me?" Jimmie joked to Luis.

Luis laughed.

"Come on, man," said Luis. "It's almost spring, but the days are still short. We only have a few hours until it gets dark."

"Yeah," said Jimmie. "And I've got stuff to do."

They both laughed.

Jimmie and Luis joined up with the rest of the Manatees at the practice field. The first players-only team meeting of the year was here. Finally.

When Luis got there, everybody stopped what they were doing.

"Hey, captain," said Roberto.

"Hey, captain," said Anthony.

"Hey, captain," said several other players.

"Hey, everybody," said Luis. "It's good to see everyone again. Are you all ready to get started? Eyes up!"

"Eyes up!" everyone said back.

Jimmie picked up a baseball and handed it to Luis.

"We're ready, captain," Jimmie said. "Just tell us what to do."

"First let's get to the dugout and clean up all

the wet leaves and trash to get ready for the new season," said Luis like a leader.

A few weeks later, Luis and his teammates were spread out in their dugout. It was the third inning of the first game of the year, and already it was raining.

But, in no time whatsoever, the storm passed. Now they were almost ready to play baseball again.

As the Manatees began to take the field, Luis stopped and looked around at his teammates.

"What's up, captain?" asked Jimmie.

"Yeah, captain," said Gary. "What's going on?"

Aliyah, Lisa and Roberto were there, too, looking back at Luis.

"I just figured out why Coach Joe makes us say 'eyes up,'" said Luis.

"It's because he wants us to be ready in case the ball comes to us, right?" said Aliyah.

"Yes," said Luis. "But it also means he wants us to have a positive attitude. You know, like, keep your head up. Stay positive. Things like that."

"Really?" said Jimmie.

"Yeah, really?" said Gary.

"Yes," said Luis. "I'm sure of it."

No one said anything for a bit.

"I think this is probably going to be a really fun year," said Luis.

"Yeah," said Jimmie.

"For sure," said Aliyah.

"It definitely is," said Gary.

And then they all jogged out onto the field together.

From the moment he first laid eyes on him, Luis knew he wasn't going to like Jimmie. But then they got to know each other, and they—along with the rest of their teammates—became good friends as they learned how to build a team.